Blessings !!

Joan Hughes

PRECIOUS *Pearl*

Written by Joan Hughes
Illustrated by Rebecca Gavney Driscoll

LITTLE CREEK PRESS™
A DIVISION OF KRISTIN MITCHELL DESIGN, LLC

Mineral Point, Wisconsin USA

Little Creek Press®
A Division of Kristin Mitchell Design, LLC
5341 Sunny Ridge Road
Mineral Point, Wisconsin 53565

Illustrator: Rebecca Gavney Driscoll
Editor: Diane Franklin
Book Design and Project Coordination: Little Creek Press

Limited First Edition
June 2014

Printed in Wisconsin, United States of America.

For more information or to order books: www.littlecreekpress.com

To contact the author, please write:
Joan Hughes
N1245 Honey Creek Road
Monroe, WI 53566

Library of Congress Control Number: 2014939919

ISBN-10: 0989978052
ISBN-13: 978-0-9899780-5-7

Dedicated to my husband Don
and children – my precious pearls,
for their love and support.

This book belongs to:

Ever since Lucy could pick up a crayon, she knew she wanted to write. When she was three years old, she made scribbles on paper and asked her mother and father to "read" what she wrote.

In kindergarten, Lucy learned how to use a pencil and write the letters of the alphabet. She was excited to learn that letters formed words and that words could be strung together to tell a story — almost like the pearls that were strung together to form the necklace that her mother wore to church every Sunday.

By the time Lucy reached fourth grade, she was stringing words together to form entertaining stories. She wrote stories about her family, stories about her friends, and stories about her pet dog, Max.

Lucy's mother said she had a gift, but it wasn't the kind of gift that came wrapped in ribbon and foil paper. Her mother explained that her gift was her talent for storytelling. This was a gift that came from God. It was a gift that became more meaningful when shared with others.

One Sunday morning, Lucy was sitting in church when she saw a tiny mouse squeeze through a hole in the wall. She could have sworn that silly mouse was looking at her during Pastor Morgan's sermon. Lucy turned her head to the side, and she was astounded to see the mouse stand on his hind legs and turn his head to the side, too.

That's how Lucy got the idea to write a story about a clever mouse that liked to imitate the people in church. The little girl in her story, whose name also was Lucy, loved to watch this amazing mouse perform. He twirled like Miss Carter, the graceful dance teacher. He yawned and stretched like Mr. Wells, the sleepy night watchman. He lowered his eyes like Miss Bridget, the shy librarian. He strutted proudly like Mr. Deaver, the richest man in town.

The Lucy in the story laughed at the mouse's antics, which made everyone in church turn toward her with disapproving looks. When Lucy tried to tell the other church-goers about the mouse, no one believed her. Surely someone else would have seen the mouse putting on a show, they said, but Lucy

explained that he liked to perform high up on the window ledge where no one else
ever looked. The pastor in the story, whose name was Pastor Jones, called Lucy into
his office and told her it was wrong to tell lies. Lucy swore that she was telling the
truth, but the Pastor didn't believe her. He did not know that a little creature was
watching from a secret hiding place.

The next Sunday, Pastor Jones delivered a sermon about the importance of telling the truth. Lucy shrunk down in her seat because she knew Pastor Jones was talking to her. The little mouse knew, too. He decided he had to help his friend. Quickly, the mouse scurried from his hiding place. He ran up the side of the pulpit and climbed onto the pastor's shoulder. Everyone in the church could see him except for Pastor Jones.

Pastor Jones liked to use his hands when he talked, so the mouse used his hands, too. The pastor raised his finger to emphasize a point, so the mouse raised his finger, too. Pastor Jones was shocked when everyone began to laugh. He scratched his head in confusion, so the mouse scratched his head, too. The befuddled pastor couldn't understand what was so funny. Then, he turned his head and saw the mouse perched on his shoulder. Pastor Jones' eyes widened. He tripped over his feet as he tried to get away from the harmless little mouse.

The mouse leaped onto the pulpit and gave the congregation a gentlemanly bow. The church-goers jumped to their feet in applause. Lucy cried with joy, and Pastor Jones never doubted her truthfulness again.

As luck would have it, the real-life Lucy got a chance to read her story in school the very next day. Lucy's new teacher, Mrs. Wellington, gave her students an assignment. She asked everyone to write a story and then stand in the front of the classroom to read it out loud. Lucy had left her story at home, so she quickly wrote it again. She raised her hand to let Mrs. Wellington know that she was ready to read it.

"Lucy, did you really write that story?" she asked.

"Yes," Lucy answered. "It's a story about a mouse who lives in my church."

Mrs. Wellington frowned. "A real mouse?"

"Yes," Lucy replied again. "He doesn't do everything the mouse in the story can do, but he's still very smart."

"I'm sorry, Lucy," Mrs. Wellington said. "I don't believe there is a real mouse. I don't believe you wrote this story. You copied it from someplace else, didn't you?"

"No. It's my story," Lucy insisted.

"It's wrong to lie, Lucy," Mrs. Wellington said with the stern look still on her face. "I will have to call your mother to discuss this."

Tearfully, Lucy returned to her seat. She felt ashamed and embarrassed, even though she had done nothing wrong. The other students in the class took turns reading their stories, but Lucy was too upset to listen.

Behind her, Lucy heard someone whisper, "Your story is the best in the class. It deserves an A+."

Lucy turned around and saw the new boy in school, Ted, smiling at her. "Didn't you hear Mrs. Wellington?" she whispered back. "She thinks I copied it. She's going to give me an F."

"She's wrong, just like Pastor Jones in your story was wrong," Ted answered. "The Lucy in the story didn't lie, and neither did you."

"How do you know?" Lucy asked.

"I see you at church each Sunday," Ted said. "I know you'd never lie. You didn't copy that story, but it must be really, really good if Mrs. Wellington thinks you did. That's why it deserves an A+."

Lucy turned forward and listened as the other students read their stories. Ted was right. Her story really was the best in class. Lucy had done such a good job that Mrs. Wellington couldn't believe a fourth-grader had written it. Suddenly, Lucy felt happy. It didn't matter what grade Mrs. Wellington gave her. Ted had said the perfect thing to turn Lucy's attitude around.

After school, Lucy's mother came in to see Mrs. Wellington with the original version of Lucy's story. The original story had crossed-out words and eraser marks, which was enough to prove that Lucy had written it. When Mrs. Wellington realized she was wrong, she apologized to Lucy and her mother.

"I'm sorry I ever doubted you, Lucy," Mrs. Wellington said. "Not many fourth-graders can write a story like that. It deserves an A+."

The next morning, Lucy hurried into the classroom and told Ted that she was going to get an A+ after all.

"That's great," Ted answered. He seemed almost as happy as Lucy was. He slid a small box across his desk toward her. "I was going to give you this to make you feel better after getting an F, but now I want you to have it for doing such a good job with your story."

Lucy opened the box. Inside was a silver bracelet with ten charms showing the Ten Commandments. "Thank you," Lucy said. "It's beautiful."

Ted smiled. "I knew with your story, you did not disobey the ninth commandment: 'Thou Shalt Not Lie.'"

On Sunday, Lucy wore her new bracelet to church while her mother wore her pearl necklace. She and Ted waved at each other as they took their seats with their families. Ted smiled when he realized that she was wearing the bracelet he had given her.

During his sermon, Pastor Morgan told the congregation the parable of the priceless pearl. He quoted a passage from scripture: "Again, the kingdom of heaven is like a merchant in search of fine pearls, who, on finding one pearl of great value, went and sold all that he had and bought it." (Matthew 13: 45-46)

That's when Lucy realized that she was blessed with fine pearls in her life that were more precious than the pearls on her mother's necklace. She remembered what her mother told her about her storytelling being a gift that was meant to share with others. An even greater gift is friendship, and that is what Ted had shared with her. By extending his friendship, Ted had turned Lucy's sorrow into joy. He had helped her have a positive outlook about her story, and that was something she would never forget.

Lucy bowed her head and said a prayer, thanking the Lord for the pearls He had given her. As she lifted her head, Lucy saw the little church mouse scurry from his hole in the wall. Lucy smiled as she realized that he had given her a gift as well. She leaned down to get closer to him and could have sworn that silly mouse was looking straight at her again.

"Thanks for the A+," she whispered.

The End

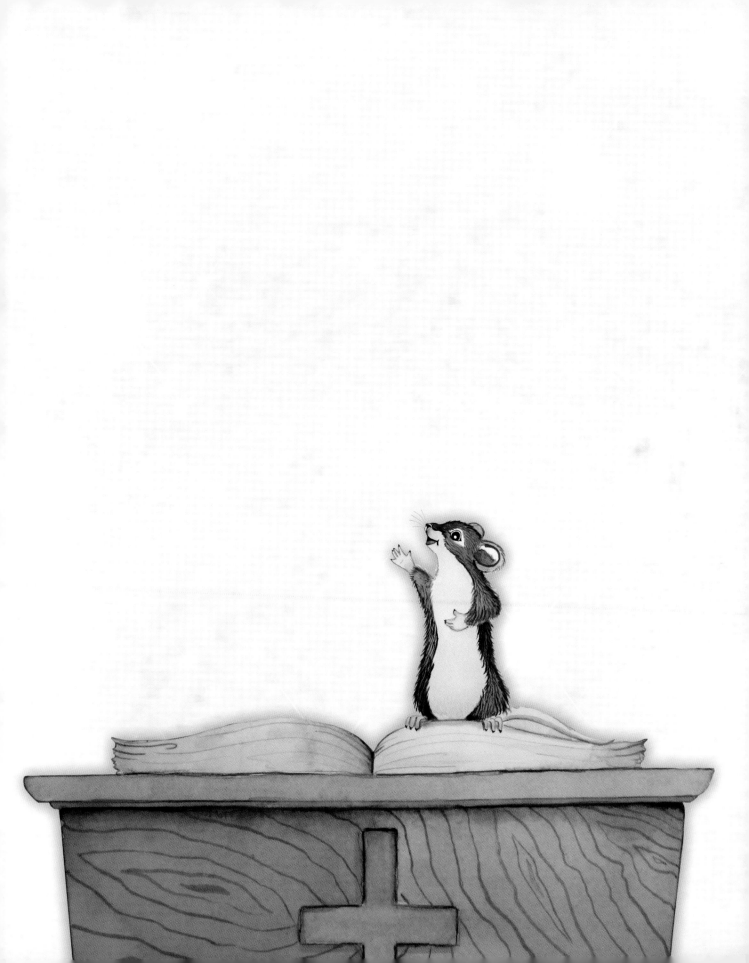

ABOUT THE AUTHOR
Joan Hughes

Joan Hughes is a native of Mineral Point, Wisconsin. Where she also raised her two sons and three step-children. She currently resides in Monroe, Wisconsin with her husband Don and dog Sadie. She is very involved in her church in Darlington, Wisconsin (Lafayette County Christian Center). This is her first book, she hopes it will help to embrace that we should always see the pearls in all situations of life.

ABOUT THE ARTIST
Rebecca Gavney Driscoll

Rebecca Gavney Driscoll is a professional illustrator residing in the beautiful state of Wisconsin. Her love of nature has inspired her to illustrate from a very young age.

She has studied art at the UW-Wisconsin system and from there has worked with various publishers.

Rebecca lives with her husband Dan and she has a son, Andrew. She also shares her home with her dog, cats and a parrot who is always trying to help her work.

You can see more of Rebecca's work at:
www.rgavneydriscoll.com